It's Pumpkin Time!

BY **Zoe Hall**

ILLUSTRATED BY
Shari Halpern

The Blue Sky Press • An Imprint of Scholastic Inc. • New York

The Blue Sky Press

Library of Congress Cataloging-in-Publication Data
Hall, Zoe, date
It's pumpkin time! / by Zoe Hall ; illustrated by Shari Halpern.
p.   cm.
Summary: A sister and brother plant and tend their own pumpkin
patch so they will have jack-o-lanterns for Halloween.
ISBN 0-590-47833-8
[1. Pumpkin—Fiction. 2. Halloween—Fiction. 3. Jack-o-lanterns—Fiction.]
I. Halpern, Shari, ill. II. Title. III. Title: It is pumpkin time.
PZ7.H1528It   1994   [E]—dc20   93-35909   CIP   AC

12 11 10 9 8 7 6 5 4 3 2   4 5 6 7 8 9/9

Printed in the United States of America   37

First printing, September 10, 1994

Special thanks to Ellen Weeks, University of Massachusetts
Cooperative Extension System, and Jan Danforth, International
Pumpkin Association, Inc., for their expert advice on pumpkins.
If you would like to order information sheets about growing and
cooking pumpkins, you can contact the International Pumpkin
Association, Inc., at 2155 Union Street, San Francisco, California 94123.

The illustrations for this book were created
using a painted paper collage technique.
Production supervision by Angela Biola
Designed by Kathleen Westray

All summer long, my brother and I get ready for our favorite holiday.

Can you guess what it is?

Halloween!
And can you guess what we do to get ready?

We plant a jack-o'-lantern patch!

First, I turn the soil with the shovel, and my brother uses the spade to dig narrow rows, just one inch deep.

Then we drop in pumpkin seeds and cover them with soil.

We water them and wait for the sun to warm them.

Before long, the seeds grow tiny roots, and small green shoots poke up out of the ground.

The shoots grow into vines, and the vines grow longer.

Every week we water them
and pull up lots of weeds.

Soon we see buds where flowers will bloom.
The yellow flowers show us where our pumpkins
will grow.

At first the pumpkins are green and tiny,

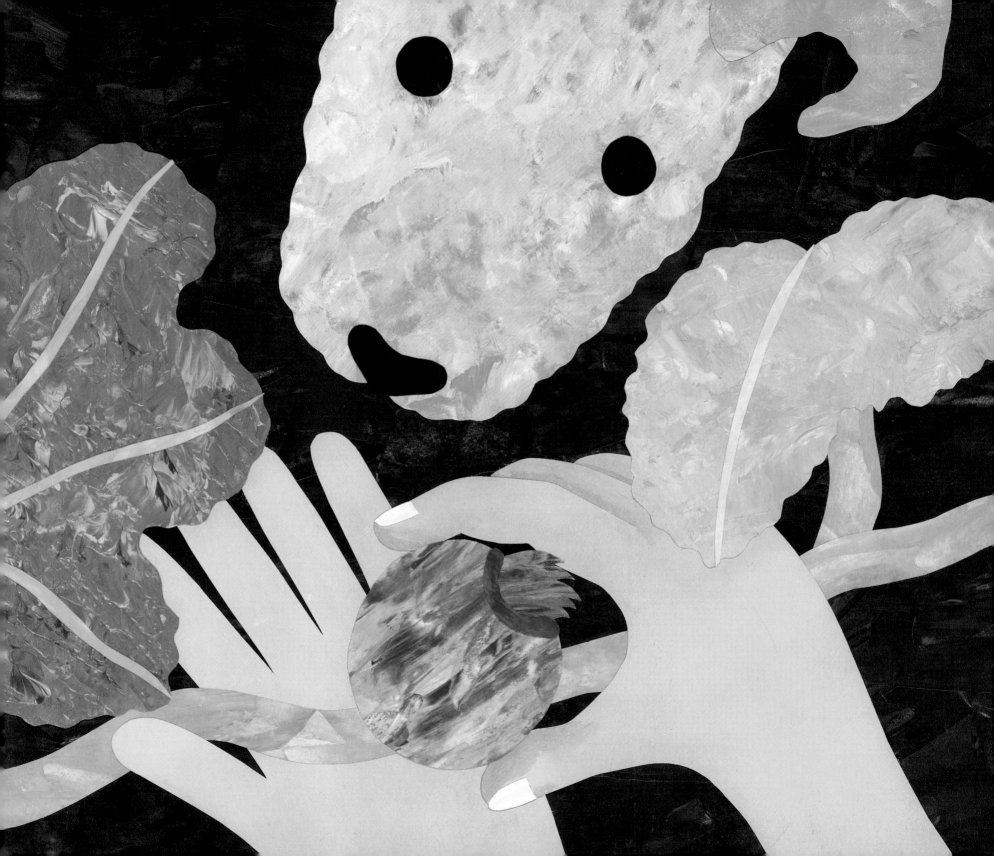

but they grow bigger

and bigger.

Soon it is fall, and our great big pumpkins change color, from green to yellow...

to orange! Now they are ready to be picked.

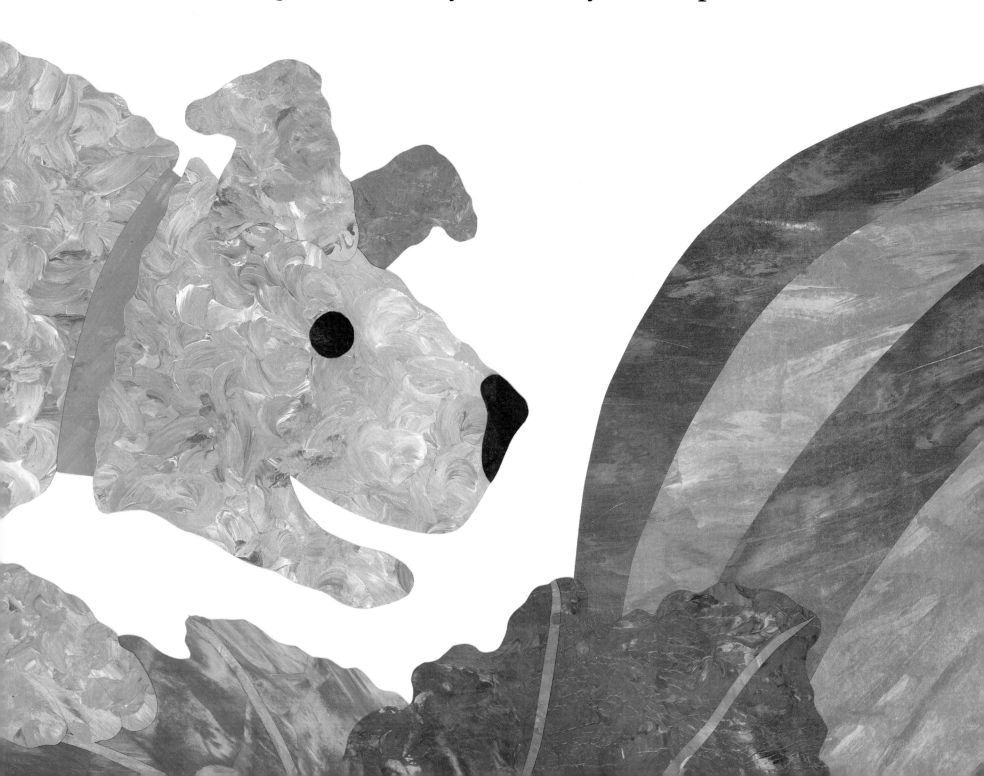

We have never grown
such big pumpkins!

Mom and Dad help us cut the pumpkins from the vines.
We gather them in a wheelbarrow and take them home.

It's Halloween at last!

We draw faces on our pumpkins,
and Mom and Dad help us cut them,
hollow them out, and light candles inside.

Now they are jack-o'-lanterns!
This one is my favorite.
Can you guess what we do next?

We put on our costumes! It's time to trick-or-treat.

Happy Halloween!

How our pumpkin seeds grow underground:

seed

1. Each **seed** is planted one inch deep in the soil.

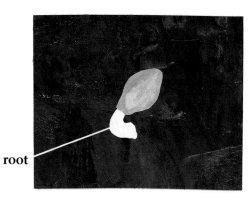

root

2. After several days, a **root** grows downward.

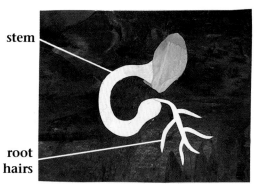

stem

root hairs

3. A **stem** starts to grow. **Root hairs** take in nutrients to help the plant grow.

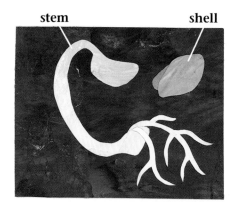

stem   shell

4. The **stem** grows upward. Inside the tip, seed leaves are tightly curled. The **shell** of the seed is left behind.

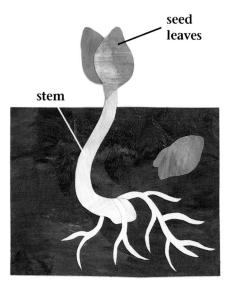

seed leaves

stem

5. The **stem** breaks through the soil. The **seed leaves** open. The shell breaks down in the soil.

pumpkin leaf

6. The first true **pumpkin leaf** grows. From now on, the plant will grow leaves with jagged edges, like this one.